Will   Irma   Taranee   Cornelia   Hay Lin

ADVENTURES

When Lightning Strikes

© 2004 Disney Enterprises, Inc.
Text copyright © 2002 by Lene Kaaberbol
W.I.T.C.H. Will Irma Taranee Cornelia Hay Lin
is a trademark of Disney Enterprises, Inc.
Volo® is a registered trademark of Disney Enterprises, Inc.
Volo/Hyperion Books for Children are imprints of
Disney Children's Book Group, L.L.C.

Printed in Singapore
First U.S. edition
1 3 5 7 9 10 8 6 4 2

This book is set in 11.5/16 Hiroshige Book.
ISBN 0-7868-0977-9
Visit www.clubwitch.com

W.i.t.c.h.

Will   Irma   Taranee   Cornelia   Hay Lin

ADVENTURES

When Lightning Strikes

By Lene Kaaberbol

VOLO

an imprint of
HYPERION BOOKS FOR CHILDREN
New York

*O*nce, long ago, when the universe was young, spirits and creatures lived under the same sky. There was only one world, only one vast realm, governed by the harmonies of nature. But evil entered the world, and found its place in the hearts and minds of spirits and creatures alike, and the world shattered into many fragments. The realm was split between those who wished for peace and those who lived to gain power over others and cause them pain. To guard and protect what was good in the worlds, the mighty stronghold of Candracar was raised in the middle of infinity.

There, a congregation of powerful spirits and creatures keep vigilance; chief among them is the Oracle. His wisdom is much needed; at times,

Candracar is all that keeps evil from entering where it should have no place.

There is also the Veil. A precious barrier between good and evil, guarded by unlikely girls.

Irma has power over water. Taranee can control fire. Cornelia has all the powers of earth. Hay Lin holds the lightness and the freedom of air. And Will, the Keeper of the Heart of Candracar, holds a powerful amulet in which all of the natural elements meet to become energy, pure and strong.

Together they are W.I.T.C.H.—five Guardians of the Veil. And the universe needs them. . . .

1

The night I met Danny Nova seemed at first such an ordinary night.

"Mom?" I called, dumping my gym bag in the hall. "I'm home."

No one answered. The apartment was empty. Well, that was not unusual. My mother works for a computer company called Simultech, and they keep her busy.

On the whole, I'm proud of my mom. She's really good at her job. And even though she's so busy, we do lots of things together. Usually, she even understands what it's like to be fourteen. As mothers go, I think she's pretty great. It's just that sometimes, coming home to an empty apartment gets kind of old.

I had been at swim practice. My hair was still damp and smelled like chlorine, and my stomach wanted something other than the lukewarm soda I had downed on the way home. I flicked on the lights in the kitchen, got a few slices of bread, and headed for the toaster.

The refrigerator cleared its throat.

"Ahem . . . Miss Will?"

I don't know whether your refrigerator ever talks to you. Mine does it all the time. It has done so ever since I found out I was a Guardian of the Veil. My element is energy, and I have this special relationship with anything electrical.

"Yes, James?" I said.

"There's a salad on my second shelf. Healthy, nutritious, full of vitamin C . . ."

"Oh. Um, thank you," I said. "But I really just want some toast and jam."

A sigh came from James's top vent. "Of course, Miss Will. Very nice, I'm sure. But allow me to point out that, of the major food groups, only one is adequately represented in the meal you propose, and a number of studies indicate a connection between—"

"All right, all right. I'll eat the salad!" I said.

"A wise choice, I'm sure," James replied.

A certain smugness had crept into his voice, but I wasn't quite through with him.

"*After* I've had my toast," I added.

The toaster chortled to herself and began to hum. It sounded a lot like: *she likes me best, she likes me best*, but Frida is not the most articulate appliance in the house, so I couldn't be sure.

James sighed again—a decidedly martyred sigh this time.

"Very well, Miss Will," James said. "I was only attempting to offer a modicum of nutritional advice."

If you think humans can sound self-righteous, then you've never met a refrigerator with a butler complex. Nobody does that here-I-am-working-day-in-day-out-with-only-her-best-interests-at-heart-and-see-where-it-gets-me routine better than my refrigerator, James. With him around, it's pretty much like having two mothers.

Frida popped the slices of toast into the air with a little too much enthusiasm. Of course, popping toast is what toasters do, but flipping the slices into a double loop and then catching them again as they come down is showing off, if you ask me.

"She likes me best, she likes me best. . . ." she continued to chant.

James harrumphed. I put my toast on a plate and then scouted his insides for the butter.

"Saturated animal fats? That would be third shelf from the top in the back, Miss Will," he said, in a voice completely frosted over with chill disapproval.

"Oh, stop sulking," I said, beginning to butter one slice. "I *said* I'd eat some salad, didn't I?"

"That is hardly the—" he began. And then his voice cut off abruptly, as all the lights went out.

Somewhere else in the building, two burglar alarms began to wail. Inside the apartment, however, the silence was deep and disturbing.

"James?" I said, hesitantly. "James, are you okay?"

It was a long time before he answered. Then, dimly, his lights came back on, and he spoke up, in a frail, slightly indignant tone.

"That's the third time this week," he complained. "How is a person supposed to work under such circumstances? Don't blame *me* if the milk goes sour."

I breathed a sigh of relief and actually patted his door with the hand that wasn't holding the half-buttered toast.

"I'm sorry, James," I said. "I realize it can't be very comfortable for you. The Heatherfield Power and Water Company says they're working on it. They're just not sure what's causing it, yet." I had heard that on the news. There had been a series of major power shortages during the past week. One of them had happened in the middle of the morning rush hour. With all the traffic signals down, central Heatherfield had been gridlocked, with honking traffic, for nearly an hour, and *nobody* had been pleased.

"You carbohydrate-consuming organisms just don't realize what it's like to be dependent on the purer forms of energy," James ranted. "You just flip a switch and expect us to function regardless. On-off, on-off. The way you treat us, anyone would think we were just machines."

"I know, James," I said soothingly. "I am very sorry."

"I've got a life, too, you know!" James said. "I've got a household to run!"

"Of course. Look, maybe you shouldn't be talking so much right now, with the power still off. You know it makes you tired. . . ." The only reason he was working at all, I knew, was because I was nearby. Well, the Heart of Candracar and I. Together, I suppose you could call us one of the strongest energy sources in the universe.

"Oh, excuse me, Miss Will," said James, in a voice dripping with injured feelings. "Do let me know if I'm boring you. Perhaps you'd rather talk with the toaster? Or with those two infernal din-makers out in the hall?"

The "din-makers" he was referring to were the still-wailing burglar alarms. Battery-powered, of course, and programmed to react to any interference with their systems. I hardly ever talked to alarms; they were such shrill, paranoid creatures, convinced everyone was out to get them. But, at that moment, James was dangerously close to sounding like that himself.

"You know, James," I said, "nobody caused these power cuts just to annoy—"

There was a knock on the door. I stopped in midsentence and dropped the slice of toast I was holding.

"Turn off!" I whispered. "Someone's at the door."

"If my services are no longer desired—" James began in an affronted tone.

"Don't be silly! Of they are. But don't you think it will strike our visitor as just a little bit odd that you're the only functioning refrigerator in downtown Heatherfield? Just . . ." I cast around for a word that would soothe his ruffled feelings, and found one. "Just be *discreet*. You do that very well!"

James smiled loftily. Don't ask me how a

refrigerator can smile—he just can. His vent sort of bends in the middle.

"Discretion is my middle name," he said, and turned himself off.

I went to answer the door.

Guardians are supposed to have feelings about the future. Instincts that tell them when to avoid a certain place, or when not to do a certain thing. Well, if I had had any such instincts, they should have been screaming as loudly as those hysterical burglar alarms: *Don't open the door! Don't open the door!* But they didn't. Not a squeak. Not a single warning.

And so, I opened the door and let Danny Nova into my life.

He didn't look so special at first. But then again, I could barely see him in the dimness of the hall. A little taller than me, maybe a little older. Or at least, that was what I thought at first.

"Sorry to burst in like this," he said politely. "But the lights went out . . . and I just moved in, and I don't even have a flashlight. Do you think I could borrow some candles?"

He had a nice voice. Full of life, somehow. And although I couldn't really see his face, there was a smile in that voice, as if he were laughing a little at his own helplessness.

"Come on in," I heard myself say. "I am pretty sure that we've got some in a drawer somewhere."

"Great. Thank you!" he said.

He followed me into the kitchen. I fumbled around until I'd found some matches and a few candles, one of which I lit.

"Oh," he said, in what sounded like absolute surprise. "I like your *hair*."

My hair? What about my hair? Had I suddenly acquired some new and radical hairstyle without meaning to? Nervously, I twisted a strand of it around my finger.

"Why?" I burst out, desperate to know what was wrong.

"It's *lightning*-colored," he said.

My hair is red. Not white, or bluish, or whatever color lightning is. Red lightning? Crazy. And then it hit me. *He likes my hair.* He wasn't being sarcastic. He wasn't being snide. He had taken one good look at my stupid red hair, and liked it.

I felt heat rise in my face. No doubt my cheeks matched my "lightning-colored" hair by now. Helplessly scarlet. Thank goodness for the dim light.

"Here," I said, "Candles." I felt extra clumsy,

holding the candles out as if I were about to start prodding him with them.

"Thank you," he said, reaching for the candles. For a brief moment, his hand covered mine. And I felt it like . . . like a small electric shock, from the top of my head to the soles of my feet. Stupid, I thought. Come on. He touched your hand, no big deal. He might not have even done it on purpose. Yet I couldn't help looking at him. I tried to make it casual, and not stare at him as if I meant to be able to describe him for a police report afterward. But I think that I probably did stare.

Danny was a little taller than me. He had auburn hair, a little curly, but not too much. His shoulders were sort of square and strong-looking, and he had perfect skin. His eyes were his best feature. They were the most incredible, electric blue, snapping with energy.

"Do you think I could have a few matches as well?" he asked.

"Er . . . sure," I stuttered. "Of course."

I turned, reaching for a book of matches.

Crunch. A loud, dry sound filled the silence. I had stepped on the toast I had dropped earlier.

"What's that?" he asked.

"I . . . er, I was making some toast." I blinked,

and pulled even more nervously at the lock of hair twined around my finger. "Would you like some?"

He eyed the mess on the floor dubiously.

"To . . . to eat?" he asked, looking at the crumbs beneath my shoe. "No, thank you. I'm . . . well, I've already eaten."

I looked down at the crumbly remains of partly buttered toast. I didn't mean *that* piece, I wanted to say. I could make you another slice. I could make you dinner. I could . . .

Oh, shut up, I told myself. Don't say it. Don't make a total idiot of yourself. All he said was that he liked your hair.

"So, you just moved in?" I finally managed to say, without blushing too hard.

"Last week. Apartment 26-B. Just down the hall. My name is Danny Nova." He held out his hand for me to shake. Hesitating just a bit, I took it. This time, there was no shock. Just the tiniest of tingles.

"I'm Will," I said. "Will Vandom. Which school do you go to?" I hadn't seen him at the Sheffield Institute yet, but a girl could always hope. . . .

"School? Oh, that's not . . . that's not quite sorted out yet. Right now, I'm on my own for a while. Where do you go to school?"

"Sheffield Institute." See? I told myself. That's not so hard. You say something. He says something. It's called having a conversation.

"Is that a nice school?" he asked.

I shrugged. "It's okay. I've got some good friends there."

"Friends are important," he said, and smiled at me.

At that moment, the power came back. Lights flickered back on, and an annoying beep from the answering machine announced that our message needed to be rerecorded.

In the brightly lit kitchen, he still looked very cute. I, on the other hand, was very conscious that my hair resembled a damp haystack.

He held out the candles. "Guess I won't need these after all."

"Keep them," I told Danny. "These power outages have been a pain for more than a week now. You never know when the next one will happen."

"Then I'd better not make off with your whole supply." He gently blew out the candle I was still holding, and solemnly divided the rest into two even piles.

There was a buzz from the apartment intercom near the front door. My mother's voice cut through the now silent room.

"Will? Are you there, sweetie?" Her voice came through the small box by the door. "I've got some stuff that needs carrying. Can you give me a hand?"

Oh. Right now? I thought. Talk about bad timing!

"I have to get going," Danny said, waving his share of the candles. "I'll see you around."

He was halfway out the door before I had time to say anything. Then his head popped back in for a second.

"You really do have *amazing* hair," he said. And then he quickly disappeared.

Amazing hair? I touched my stringy, wet, and chlorinated head. No accounting for taste, I decided. Slowly, I pressed the intercom button.

"Hi, Mom." I said. "I'm coming down."

"Thanks, sweetie," she answered.

But for a little while I just stood there, remembering the small shock I had felt when he had first touched my hand. Electricity. I had heard people talk about it, but I had never thought they meant it so literally.

"Miss Will?"

"Yes, James?"

There was a long, strange pause, as if he wanted to say something, but didn't know quite how to put it. I simply waited.

"Don't forget to eat your salad, Miss," he finally muttered. But I had a weird feeling that that wasn't what he had *meant* to say at all.

And so that was how I met Danny Nova. The Boy Next Door. A very ordinary meeting, really, compared to what followed.

2

*B*oom, *boom. Boom-boom-boom.* A thumping bass line echoed deafeningly across the parking lot. A crowd of students on their way home had gathered to watch some people dance.

"Who's that?" asked Taranee, craning her neck for a better glimpse.

"I don't know," I said. "Look, we'd better get going. My mom said she'd be home early today."

There was a wild, whooping cheer from the crowd, and a smattering of applause.

"Awesome!" someone yelled.

"Don't you want to see what's going on?" said Taranee. More and more students were joining the crowd, and the clapping had gotten loud and rhythmic. "Come on, Will, it'll only take a minute."

I shrugged. "Okay." I had to admit, I was

starting to get curious myself.

Three boys were dancing. Two of them were from Sheffield; I didn't know their names, but I had seen them around. They were good dancers and knew some really cool moves, but they weren't the reason for the crowd. It was the third boy that everyone was looking at. He was spinning and sliding with the beat of the music, precisely in time with the hammering bass, the pounding percussion. His whole body seemed to *pulse* to the beat. It *was* awesome to look at, just as the guy in the crowd had just said. And it was Danny doing it, Danny, my new neighbor from practically next door.

"Wow," breathed Taranee. "He's *good*."

I nodded silently, and watched as Danny gave a whole new meaning to the term "moving to the beat."

The music came to an end. The two Sheffield boys were puffing and sweating, with damp stains on their T-shirts and a sheen on their faces. Danny didn't even look out of breath.

Then he saw me. His face lit up in a delighted grin.

"Will!" he called. "I was hoping to catch you."

Everyone turned to see who he was talking to. Suddenly a whole crowd of people were looking right at me. I bit my lip and fingered my hair nervously. "Hi, Danny."

Taranee gave me a look. "You *know* him?" she whispered in awe.

"New neighbor," I whispered back, out of the side of my mouth.

Danny moved closer to me.

"Can we . . . go somewhere?" Danny asked. "The park? The mall? You could show me around."

"Yes," I said, instantly. Then I remembered that Taranee had promised to help me with my math that afternoon. "That is, er . . . Taranee . . . you don't mind, right?" I gave her a pleading look.

She heaved a sigh. "Oh, all right. I'll come by later. Seven?"

"You're the best." I gave her arm a light, grateful punch. Before Taranee walked away, she gave me a smile and a wink. And then, of course, I stood there like an idiot, not knowing what to do next. "Where do you want to go?" I finally asked him.

Danny eyed the stereo that one of the Sheffield boys was hoisting onto his shoulder. "Maybe you could show me where to get one of those," he said. "I would really like that."

I was surprised he didn't have one already. Guys who danced the way he did usually practiced anytime, anywhere, in the mall, in parking lots, or on any street corner.

"Sure," I said. "We can go to the Honeydew Center. There are several good shops there."

As we walked off, I could hear some of the students talking behind us.

"Who was that guy?" a girl with blond hair asked.

"I don't know," said one of the other dancers. "He just came up, looked at us for a while, and then joined in. He had the moves, though."

"You got that right!" the blond girl said.

I looked back. The crowd was scattering now that the show was over. But one guy still stood there, watching Danny and me walk away.

Matt Olsen.

There wasn't really anything between Matt Olsen and me. He had been nice to me a couple of times, that was all. He was the kind of guy who was nice to everyone. I was the one who thought *he* was cute, not the other way around. I was the one with the major crush. So why did I get this stupid pang of guilt?

I gave a small, embarrassed wave of my hand. Matt waved back. Then he got on his bike and rode off. And I took Danny to the Honeydew Center, to look at stereos.

☾ ☾ ◬ ☉ ☾

"So," said Taranee, dumping her math books on my desk later that night. "How did it go?"

"How did what go?" I asked, flopping onto my bed.

"Your date," Taranee said, sitting down next to me. She clearly wasn't at my house just to study. She wanted the scoop on the afternoon.

"It wasn't a date, Taranee," I explained. "I was just showing him around."

"Oh, sure," she said.

I played with the fur on my stuffed green frog. "Danny is new here," I told Taranee.

"Obviously," said Taranee, pushing her glasses up on her nose.

"I was only being . . . neighborly," I said. I began twirling my hair around my finger.

"Hmmm . . ." Taranee eyed me in the way only a best friend could.

"Taranee!" I said.

"What?" she asked, innocently.

"Stop looking at me like that!" I protested.

Taranee grinned. "You twirl that any harder, and you'll lose some hair."

I let go of the lock of hair that I had been

winding around my finger. I don't do it all the time, only when I'm feeling embarrassed.

"He is a very cool dancer, and he looks just like JoeJoe," Taranee commented.

JoeJoe's new single, *I Got the Power*, was currently featured on the cover of every music magazine that considered itself cutting-edge.

"He does look a lot like that," I murmured. "But he's not . . . I mean, we're not . . . I'm not really . . . I was just . . ."

"Uh-oh," said Taranee, smiling. "You've got it bad."

"Stop teasing me!" I shouted.

Taranee became serious for a moment. "Will, this isn't like you," she said.

"What isn't like me?" I asked. "The fact that a boy actually likes me?"

"Don't be so touchy," Taranee said. She got up off the bed and went over to her book bag. "You know that's not what I meant. I just think you're better off with Matt, that's all."

"Yes, well, the trouble is, I'm not *with* Matt, in case you hadn't noticed," I explained. "Danny, on the other hand, is actually aware that I'm alive. He even seems to like me. And being with him is *fun*, Taranee. Is that such a crime?"

"No," she said, shaking her head so hard that

the tiny beads in her braids clinked.

"Okay, then." I opened the math book. "Look, can you explain this square-root whatsit to me? That would be really useful."

"Mmm . . ." Taranee sighed. But she didn't begin her explanation, at least not right away. Instead, she kept looking at me with this odd, worried expression on her face.

"What is it?" I finally asked.

She sighed. "Promise you won't get mad?"

It was my turn to sigh. "You're one of my best friends and my fellow Guardian. When do I ever get mad at you?" I thought about that for a moment. "Seriously mad, I mean."

"It's just . . ." she said, "I'm not sure that Danny's safe."

"Safe? Oh, please, Taranee." I exclaimed. "What is he going to do? Carry me off to some dungeon? Feed me to his pet monster?"

"Don't say that," snapped Taranee. "Even as a joke. You know weird stuff sometimes happens to us."

That much was true. It sort of came with being a Guardian of the Veil. Sometimes it felt as if the five of us, Taranee and I, and Irma, Cornelia, and Hay Lin, were all wearing signs on our backs that read: *Trouble, please line up here.*

You will be attended to as soon as staff is available. But Danny wasn't trouble. Danny looked far too—well, *ordinary* wasn't quite the word, but he didn't sport fangs or claws or extra heads, or any of the other special features we had had to deal with in the past.

"He's just a boy," I said. "And I'm supposed to be a Guardian. Surely I can handle one teenage dancer. Even if he does look a lot like JoeJoe."

The lights dimmed, came back on, then went out completely. There was an anguished cry from the study, where my mother had been working on her computer.

"Oh, no! I don't believe it. Not again!"

A moment later, there was a soft knock on my door.

"Will!" my mother called. "When the power comes back on, can you please do your magic computer thing? Otherwise I've just lost two hours' worth of work."

"I'll try," I said. My mom didn't mean real magic; she just thought I had somehow developed really good computer skills.

"Thanks, Will," she sighed. "Why don't you and Taranee come into the kitchen? There's some cookies, and I've lit a couple of candles. I hope Heatherfield Power and Water gets this straightened out soon, though. Otherwise, there won't be a sane computer worker left in the city."

It was nice to sit there in the dark kitchen with my mom and Taranee. I didn't mind postponing the square roots for a while. But I knew that James; Frida; George, the computer; Billy, our old television; and all of our other appliances would be frightened and uneasy. With my mom there I couldn't soothe them at all.

"It's a bit strange, isn't it?" I said, sipping my tea. "What is it now, nine or ten outages in about a week? Someone ought to do something." I caught Taranee's eye.

Taranee nodded slowly. "Yes. Someone really should look into it."

3

"It's just that too many people have air-conditioning now," said Cornelia. "And computers. And about a million other appliances that use up a lot of electricity."

"It's not hot enough yet for a lot of air-conditioning to be turned on," objected Hay Lin. "I think Will has a point. These outages aren't normal."

We were in an abandoned lot a couple of blocks from the Honeydew Center. It wasn't exactly one of the highlights on the scenic Heatherfield tour, being basically a very large hole in the ground, with a few freestanding, concrete pillars and a lot of weeds, mud, and rust-colored water. But it had the advantage of being deserted most of the time, which made it a good practice spot for us. You think Guardians don't have to practice? Think again.

"All right, then," said Irma. "What do we do about it? Ask the Oracle?"

"Oh, yeah, right," said Cornelia. "How will that look? Honored Oracle, Heatherfield Power and Water is having some trouble. Could you kindly help them out? That is, if you are not too busy watching the fate of all the universe."

Put like that, it did sound like a very small problem to bother the Oracle with.

"In any case," said Cornelia, "He'd probably only tell us to fix it ourselves. He usually does."

Cornelia said this with a certain pride, and I couldn't help smiling myself. It was true that the Oracle rarely interfered directly, but somehow, he always made us feel that, if we would only do our very best, we could solve even the most impossible-looking problems.

"At least, after we've talked to him, we know what it is we're supposed to be fixing," said Taranee. "If these aren't natural power shortages, I have no idea what they are, or why they're happening."

"Will . . . can't you ask it?" said Irma.

I frowned. "Electricity, you mean? The power itself? I could try, but . . . electricity doesn't really have a memory. When it's there, it's there, and when it's gone, it's gone. On. Off. I'd have more luck asking . . . oh, I don't know, one of the transformers at the power station, maybe. I don't know how we'd get in, though."

"Maybe they have tours," said Hay Lin.

"I'll find out," said Taranee. "Now, do we practice or not? It's getting late."

What we do during our practice sessions varies. Sometimes we try to get our elements to work together on complicated things like astral drops. That's a really neat and somewhat scary trick where we create a sort of double for one of us, or doubles for all of us. We need to do that when we leave Heatherfield and go to Metamoor so that no one realizes that we have left. Looking at the astral drop is like looking at yourself—that's the freaky part. The drops move like us, talk like us—or at least they do if we've done it right. I once made one that did just about *everything* wrong; but that's a whole other story.

Other times, we try to spring surprises on each other. If you are attacked, you have to be able to react quickly—especially if the attack is physical. And believe me, we have been attacked often enough to know we need the practice. So, like boxers, I guess, we spar.

Which is why, half an hour later, I found

myself being lifted into the air by a huge water-spout that then proceeded to hold me there, like a Ping-Pong ball in a fountain.

"Okay, Irma," I said. "You've made your point. Now, let me down."

She didn't. She was too busy rolling on the ground, laughing her head off.

"I'm getting wet," I said. As a matter of fact, I was getting *very* wet. And it was still very cold. Plus, I don't really like heights that much.

Irma was still giggling like mad and showed no sign of putting a stop to her column of water. Enough was enough. I called the Heart of Candracar into my hand.

It's in me, or with me, all the time. But when I want it to be visible, it looks like a crystal pendant, glowing with pure light. The Heart is what unites us. In it, all the natural elements—water, fire, air, and earth—come together as pure energy. I supposed that that ability to unite, to merge, and to meld, was what made me the leader of W.I.T.C.H. And I was about to remind Irma of that important fact.

I couldn't, and wouldn't, attack her with the Heart. But I could bar her from using the powers the Heart gave her. Without them, Irma would still have *some* magic, but she wouldn't be as strong.

As the Heart began to glow blue and green, Irma's column of water sank gently back into the earth and became a mere trickle. And I landed, very cold and wet, on the muddy ground.

Irma stopped laughing.

"Sorry," she said. "I got a little carried away. But the look on your face . . ."

"Oh, ha-ha," I said. "Very funny." I was beginning to shiver.

Taranee gently touched my wet sleeve. "Just a second," she said, screwing up her face in concentration. My clothes began to steam. A few moments later they were dry. They still smelled a little funny, like something that's been in your gym bag for too long, but I was a lot warmer. That was one of the advantages of having a Guardian with power over fire for a friend.

Irma gave me a hug. "Sorry. Real sorry. Can we be friends again? Please?" She made herself go cross-eyed—she's very good at being goofy. "Please-please-please-please-please?" Irma can be a big drama queen.

I could never stay angry at Irma for very long. She makes me laugh too much to be mad. I grinned.

"Oh, all right," I said. I glared at her. "Wicked water witch that you are."

I opened the Heart to her once more. Irma sighed contentedly as the full powers of her element came back to her.

"That's better," she said. "This is more like *me*."

The sky was beginning to darken, and streetlights were starting to come on.

"Time to go home," said Hay Lin. "Better hide the Heart again, Will."

There was a movement in the shadows that startled us all and drew a breathless gasp from Taranee. "Wow! What a weird cat! Did you ever see one that big?"

The cat was already gone, a maroon streak, lightning-quick. I let the Heart disappear from sight, grateful that our surprise visitor was only an animal.

"More like a small panther," said Cornelia. "Look at the size of those paw prints!"

"Just think how many cans of cat food his owner has to drag home every week," giggled Irma. "The poor guy must have a permanent hernia."

Then I realized there had been something odd about the cat, other than its size.

"Did you ever see a cat with eyes like that?" I asked. "With eyes that blue?"

Irma shrugged. "Siamese, maybe," she said. "Forget the cat. I'm hungry. Who wants to share a pizza on the way home?"

€ ℮ ⬠ ◉ ℮

The next day, just after I had come home from school, there was an energetic knock at the door. It was Danny.

"Can you come over?" he asked. "I've got something to show you!"

I followed Danny down the hall to his apartment. The something turned out to be a brand-new stereo, along with a row of CDs.

"You bought it!" I said, checking out the new, high-tech set we had seen the other day in the store. "Great. What did your parents say?"

"Oh, they're not . . . they're still traveling," Danny said. "They won't be back for another couple of weeks."

"You're on your own?" I said, faintly surprised. Not that he didn't look as if he could take care of himself, but it was still . . . a bit unusual.

His apartment was a bit unusual, too. I knew he had just moved in, but even so, it was totally bare. Apart from the stereo and his new CDs, there were a chair that looked as if it had been left behind by the previous occupant and a pile of newspapers and magazines. I noticed that one of them had JoeJoe on the cover.

Danny put a CD into the stereo and pressed the PLAY button. JoeJoe's voice echoed through the bare flat.

I got the power, I got the moves, I got the music, I got the grooves. . . .

Danny had begun to dance. "Come on," he said, waggling his fingers at me. "Isn't this great stuff?"

"Yes, but . . ." I stood there, feeling completely awkward. "I don't . . . dance that well."

"Who cares?" Danny said, with a smile. "Come on. I'll teach you some moves."

He grinned at me again, and it was such a *nice* grin. A you-can-do-anything grin. A this-is-just-for-fun grin.

"Come on, Lightning Girl," he said. And suddenly I didn't care that I wasn't the world's best dancer. What he was doing looked like fun. I tried to copy him. I didn't quite succeed. Danny laughed, and that made me giggle. I tried again, feeling a little more comfortable. By the end of the song, I was dancing. Well, sort of.

"One more?" he asked, his eyes sparkling.

Well, why not? I thought. I was dancing with the hottest new boy in school. And I was having a great time.

We danced for nearly two hours. By the end of it, I was breathless and feeling pretty tired from all the exercise.

"I think I could learn to like this," I said.

"You should," Danny told me. "You're already really good." He looked at me and I thought I was going to melt.

I looked regretfully at my watch.

"I have to go now," I said. "My mom will be home any minute, and I promised I'd have dinner with her tonight."

Right before I got to the door, Danny called out to me.

"Wait," he said. "Are you free tomorrow?"

I stopped, my hand on the doorknob. "Um . . ." I stumbled. I felt my face going into major blush mode! But I wanted to see Danny again. "When?" I finally managed to say.

"Tomorrow night?" Danny asked. He looked incredibly cute as he gazed at me hopefully. "You've been so nice to me, showing me around and everything. I'd like to take you out some-where. How about Carnival Bay? Would you like that?"

Oh, I thought. This sounds like a date. A real, honest-to-goodness date. With Danny. Would I like that? Everything was happening so fast!

"Thanks," I said. "Yes, I'd . . . like that very much."

His face lit up with that irresistible smile of his, brimming with cheerfulness and energy.

"Great!" he said. He stood at the door watching as I walked down the hall. Actually, I felt as if I were floating!

€ € ◭ ◉ ⦿

The next morning, while I was standing at my locker getting out my books for first period, Matt appeared, taking me totally by surprise.

"My grandpa has dumped a litter of puppies on us," he said. Matt's grandfather, Mr. Olsen, owned a pet shop. Sometimes I worked there after school. Of course, I had started working there because I wanted to see more of Matt. But Matt had never seemed to notice whether I was there or not. I did like being at the shop, in any case, and Mr. Olsen was really a nice man.

"Um . . . oh . . ." I said, not very intelligently.

"Spaniels," he said. "Fur so soft and silky you wouldn't believe it. I was wondering. . . . would you like to come by and see them?"

"Um . . . when?" I asked.

"Tonight, if you're free," Matt stood there asking me that question as if he were part of a scene from one of my daydreams. I couldn't believe it.

Oh, no.

"Um . . . I can't," I said. "I've got . . . that is, I have to . . . I'm really sorry. . . ." I couldn't believe what I was saying.

Matt shrugged. "Hey," he said. "It's no big deal. I just thought you'd like to see them."

I would, I thought. Ask me again. Tomorrow night. Any other night. Please.

But he had already moved off down the hall and started laughing with some of the older girls from his own grade.

He was only being nice, I told myself. If he really wanted to see me, he wouldn't have given up so easily. He would have suggested some other night. Wouldn't he have?

I slammed my locker door closed as the buzzer rang. I should have been more upset about what was happening. But all I could think about was my date with Danny.

4

Thunder rumbled. The air around us stood absolutely still. My hair seemed to float and cling with static electricity.

"Do you think it's going to rain?" I asked.

Danny shook his head. He was looking very cute in his blue sweater and jeans.

"No," he said, sounding very certain. "No rain." He smiled at me, a brilliant, excited smile. He looked as if he could barely stand still. "Come on," he said. "There are so many *fun* things to do here!"

We were at Carnival Bay, Heatherfield's harbor-front fairground. The lighted curve of the great Ferris wheel was brilliant against the slate-gray sky, and the smell of popcorn, hot dogs, and hamburgers was overpowering.

"Look, let's try that!" Danny said. He pointed to his left.

Bumper cars. Well, why not? I thought. I used to love them. With Danny, it could be fun.

Riding a bumper car with Danny *was* fun. We were like cannonballs, flying from one end of the ring to the other, a menace to everything and everybody. Our car was much faster than anyone else's, and Danny spun the wheel with swift grace, sliding all over.

Danny laughed and whooped like a five-year-old. I couldn't help laughing, too, and at some point, even the other drivers started whooping and grinning. It was contagious—Danny was so good, and he was having such a good time, that everyone else caught part of that enthusiasm. It seemed to me that the guy in charge of the ride let us go much longer than he should have, just to watch the action.

When the ride was finally over, a few kids from the other cars shook hands with Danny and clapped him on the shoulder. Danny grinned, his eyes positively shining. I looked at him and thought that until then I had never met anyone who lived life to the fullest, as Danny did.

As we passed a concession stand I asked Danny if he wanted anything to drink.

He shook his head. "I'm not thirsty," he said. Then he was on to the next thing. He was like a little kid! "Let's go on that!" he said, pointing to the Ghost Train.

Because a thunderstorm was threatening, the fairground wasn't crowded, and we had a whole train car to ourselves. With a suitably ghostly whistle, the train took off down the first dark tunnel of what was supposed to be an abandoned mine. A sudden unseen drop made my stomach flutter, and I clutched at the bar that held me in place. Danny laughed, a nice sound, that felt as reassuring as a warm blanket.

The train labored up a steep rise—up, up, up . . . A skeleton with an ax leaped out at us, screeching, then disappeared over the edge. We followed. Cold air mixed with a scent of machine oil rushed at me, whipping back my hair. And then we turned a corner and ran into cobwebs. Startled, I brushed wildly at my face. An eerie, green light flashed and revealed a mass of cobwebs with spiders the size of softballs.

"Nice," I muttered, thinking it was lucky that Taranee—who is really afraid of spiders—wasn't here to see the sight. I wasn't scared of spiders . . . much.

Suddenly, there was a searing flash. Around us, power sparked and surged. Then, the car stopped, and all the lights went out.

Oh, no, I thought, not another power outage. Or maybe it was part of the ride? No. I had *felt* the power surge and break; I had felt it leap right . . .

. . . Into Danny.

Shock stilled my heart for a second.

"Danny?"

No answer.

"Danny, are you all right?" I fumbled for his hand. I couldn't find it. Where was he? Had he . . . had he been . . . My own hands were trembling. A current that strong could kill.

"Danny!"

Where was he? Why didn't he answer?

It was pitch-dark in the fake mine shaft. I couldn't see my hand in front of my face. I was in a total panic. I was scared—and afraid for Danny. There was only one thing that I could do.

I brought out the Heart.

The Heart's gentle glow illuminated the glistening threads of spiderweb—and an empty seat beside me.

A sound made me turn. Behind me, on the back rim of the car, stood Danny, balanced like an acrobat. For once, he wasn't smiling.

"Sorry," he said, and brought a hand up on either side of my face, quite gently.

Sorry? I thought. But . . .

And then power exploded through me, and everything went black.

�✦�△�◎�✦

"Miss? Miss, are you all right?"

The words were fuzzy, as if I were hearing them underwater. I was cold. My mouth was dry. I ached all over. What had happened?

I looked around frantically, finally realizing why I felt so awful.

Danny was gone.

And so was my Heart.

5

"*C*an we get a blanket over here? Miss, can you hear me?"

"Yes," I muttered, and tried to open my eyes. What was this . . . this horrible feeling I had? I blinked and tried to focus.

A stranger was bending over me, a stranger in a cheerful, red-and-yellow uniform. I squinted at the man's shirt pocket. CARNIVAL BAY STAFF.

Carnival Bay. Ghost Train. Danny.

"Did anyone see the boy I was with?" I asked. "He's about this tall, auburn hair, very blue eyes." I looked around anxiously at the crowd of people looking at me.

No one knew who I was talking about.

"He'll come back," said the Carnival Bay staffer who had found me. "Probably just went to get help." He looked at me pityingly. He clearly thought Danny was a creep for ditching his date. I couldn't even begin to explain that what Danny had really done was much, much worse.

Infinitely worse.

I couldn't stop shivering. I felt hollow inside.

The Carnival Bay doctor took my pulse and blood pressure and shined a small flashlight into my eyes. I told her that no, I hadn't hit my head, and no, I wasn't having trouble breathing. I just couldn't stop shivering.

"Are you by any chance claustrophobic?" the doctor asked.

I almost told her no, but then had second thoughts. The doctor didn't want to let me go without an explanation, and I couldn't tell her what had really happened. Claustrophobia would have to do.

"A little," I said, with a sigh. "Well, maybe more than a little."

The doctor put her flashlight back in her pocket. "Were you scared when the lights went out in the tunnel?"

I nodded and told myself it wasn't a complete lie—I had been scared, terribly scared that something had happened to Danny. And all the while, he had been preparing to . . . My stomach cramped at the thought, and I took a deep breath.

She stroked my arm. "Take it easy. I think I know what happened." The doctor leaned over and helped me to sit up. "You were scared enough to start hyperventilating, and you fainted," she explained. "If it ever happens again, just concentrate on your breathing. Big, slow breaths. You'll be all right."

"Thanks," I said. I wished that it were that simple. How could I explain to this doctor that Danny had just stolen the Heart of Candracar from me?

"Now, do you have someone to take you home?" the staffer from Carnival Bay asked. "You're still a bit foggy."

I assured the staff guy that I was fine. I didn't live far from there, I explained.

The doctor had told me to walk slowly, but I ran. I needed to get to Danny's apartment fast. I needed to catch that two-faced, lying *thief* before he . . .

"Will!"

Taranee, Cornelia, Irma, and Hay Lin were all waiting for me in the lobby of my building.

They all looked stunned . . . and worried.

Taranee stepped forward. "Will, what happened?" she asked.

"We all had this really awful feeling," Hay Lin

ssaid. "We came here right away."

"But when we came over, you weren't here," Irma explained.

Cornelia put her hand on my arm. "We've been waiting here for you. We didn't know where to find you. Will, what happened?"

I couldn't tell them. I just couldn't. But then I forced myself to look at their faces. I was supposed to be their leader, and I knew that I had to tell them.

"It was Danny," I said in a voice that was barely a whisper. "He . . . he stole the Heart."

€ € ⬟ ◎ €

Cornelia put her hand flat against the door to apartment 26-B. The lock went *click*—moving solid objects by wishing is sort of her specialty.

We all went inside Danny's apartment. Hay Lin shone her flashlight around the hall. No one was there. Actually, nothing was there. The place was totally empty. Well, it had been more or less empty even when Danny had been there. But now, he was obviously gone. The question was, where did he go?

"My goodness," said Cornelia a little breathlessly. "Look!"

She pointed her flashlight at what had once been an electric socket. Now it was a burnt and bubbly plastic mess. Every single electrical outlet in the apartment looked the same way.

"Oooh," Irma said as she stood in the middle of the living room. On the wall there was a large, blackened circle, about a foot wide.

"What happened?" asked Hay Lin. "What did he *do*?"

"I guess those power outages weren't Heatherfield Power and Water's fault, huh?" Irma chuckled.

"Shhh!" Taranee said to Irma, giving her a slap on the shoulder.

Some sort of light was beginning to come on in my dim brain. "I don't know why or how, but Danny *must* have had something to do with it," I said. I remembered that frightening instant when I had felt the power leap from everywhere around me *into* Danny.

"Is . . . is . . . he gone?" a very small and shaky voice asked. And the voice most definitely did not come from any of us.

I jumped. I think we all did. The beams of our two flashlights flickered like searchlights around the room.

"There," I cried. "On the windowsill!"

It was a small transistor radio. It was blue, like Danny's eyes. But I definitely did not want to think about Danny's gorgeous eyes just then.

"Did you see him go?" I asked the radio.

"He didn't even say good-bye." A bit of static and a snatch of quivering string music accompanied that statement. "Gone. Just gone. Left me. Left me *all alone*." The violin strings quivered even more.

"Where did he go?" asked Cornelia, leaning closer to the radio.

The blue radio ignored her and stuck to mournful music.

"You ask it," Cornelia said to me. "We have to know."

I nodded. "Please," I said. "It's really very important. Where did Danny go?"

"All alone. And I tried so hard," the voice was fading quickly. "But, no. I wasn't enough for him! And now he's gone off with *her*." The last word came out so scratchy I wondered whether the radio's batteries might be dying.

"Her?" I said, feeling a twinge of jealousy. "What her?"

"That great, big, vulgar, noisemaker he got!" The radio seemed to gain strength with its anger. "No class. No *culture*."

The radio must have been referring to Danny's new, high-tech CD player. Visions of

Danny laughing behind my back with some slinky-type, model-faced girl a thousand times better looking than me faded from my mind. And then I wanted to kick myself for even thinking about something so trivial when real disasters were about to come down on us. Correction: they had already come down on us—the Heart was gone.

"What happened?" I asked, gently picking the radio up in my hands.

"He turned into a light," the radio said.

"He *what*?" all of us said together.

The transistor radio continued to hum mournfully. "That's what happened. He fed himself, and then he turned into a light."

"Fed himself?" Irma asked. "What does that mean?"

"From the sockets," said the blue radio, as if that were obvious and completely reasonable. And to the radio it was, of course. The little radio, too, lived on what James usually called "the purer forms of energy." But Danny?

"You mean he . . . feeds on electricity?" I asked, just to be sure.

"Of course. And what an appetite that boy has!" If the radio had had a face, it would have been beaming.

The five of us stared at each other. We had battled some crazy creatures lately, but this situation was getting stranger and stranger.

"Well," said Hay Lin faintly, "Whatever he is, Danny certainly isn't from around here."

🌀 🌀 🌀 🌀 🌀

We sat in my room, gloomily contemplating our options. They were depressingly few.

"We have to talk to the Oracle," Hay Lin said.

I couldn't argue with that. Even though I didn't like the idea of standing before him, and the Congregation of Candracar, with all of them knowing what a fool I'd been, I knew the only option that I had was to fess up. I had to admit that I was careless. And I was a *bad* Keeper of the Heart. I felt empty and ashamed.

My pet dormouse bumped against my hand. It curled itself up in my lap and just lay there quietly, which was unusual for the little critter. The animal is usually very active for a dormouse. But right now the small, warm weight of it was a huge comfort. I stroked its soft fur gently.

"We really have to talk to the Oracle," Hay Lin said, this time a little louder.

"Hmmm . . . ," said Irma. "One snag, though. Without the Heart, how do we get there?"

Once more, we stared at each other. That

thought hadn't even occurred to me. But Irma was right. Before, when we had traveled to Candracar, or anywhere else outside our world, the Heart had always been involved.

I think it was only then that I realized the enormity of the disaster I had created. Up until that moment, I think I had just felt like a child who had done something really bad, but still thought that somehow it could all be easily fixed. But if we couldn't even *get* to the Oracle? What if we never got the Heart back? Who were we without it? And what about Candracar? Could . . . could Danny, or whoever he was, actually threaten the Oracle and the Congregation of Candracar?

"We're not even proper Guardians anymore," I whispered. Losing the Heart didn't just affect me, it affected all of us. And if the Heart were truly gone . . . I didn't even dare to think about what that could do to the balance of good and evil in the universe.

"Will . . ." Taranee's hand closed awkwardly over mine. "Don't take it so hard."

"We'll think of something," Cornelia said softly.

I don't cry very often. But I knew that if I had to sit there one second longer with everyone being nice to me, they were going to need a mop and bucket to wipe up the flood. Cradling my dormouse, I slowly got up.

"Where are you going?" Irma asked.

"I need some water," I said, choking up, and headed for the kitchen on rubbery legs.

The dormouse squirmed, and I let it go. At that moment I honestly didn't care whether the animal gnawed on every bit of upholstery in the house. I ran some cold water over my hands and then pressed them against my face.

"Miss Will?"

"Yes, James?" I answered.

"There's some chocolate on my bottom shelf," James stated.

Chocolate. My cure-all when I was feeling down. I must have looked really awful for James to suggest something so nutritionally unsound.

"Thank you," I told him.

"Would you care for some, Miss?" he asked.

"Not right now, thank you," I said and splashed more water on my face. This wasn't a crisis that could be drowned in chocolate. Actually, the thought made me feel faintly sick.

I dried my hands slowly on a kitchen towel. I dreaded going back to the others. Whoever said that misery loved company never had problems like mine. When I looked at my four friends and thought of what I'd done to them, I felt exactly four times as guilty as before. I was supposed to be the leader of the Guardians. And I had led my friends into trouble. Big trouble.

"Ahem. Miss Will?" James cleared his voice in his most butlerish fashion. "There's always the magic word, you know."

What magic word? I didn't know any spell that would have gotten back the Heart, or even taken us to Candracar. Then I realized what he meant.

"You mean . . . just say 'please'?" I asked.

He smiled faintly. "It quite often works."

Mulling it over, I went back to my room, where the others were slumped as dejectedly as before. Hay Lin and Cornelia were lying on my bed. Taranee was leaning against my desk, and Irma was swinging around in the desk chair.

"I have an idea. Sort of," I began.

They all looked up at me.

"Yeah?" said Taranee. "What is it?"

"I know we can't go to Candracar without the Heart," I said. "But what if we asked the Oracle to take us there? Asking very nicely, of course."

"You mean—you think he might be able to hear us?" Cornelia asked.

"Why not?" Taranee said. "He seems to know most of what goes on everywhere."

Irma scratched her head. "It can't hurt to try," she said.

"What do we do? Just . . . close our eyes and wish? Or what?" Hay Lin asked, sitting up a little straighter on my bed.

I shrugged. "I thought . . . maybe we could hold hands. All five of us. Do it together." Even without the Heart, I thought, we'd be stronger together.

Hay Lin slid off the bed and came to sit cross-legged on the floor beside Taranee. "Okay," she said simply.

Irma and Cornelia sat down, too. I looked around the circle. We were so different. Taranee was quiet and thoughtful, and at times a little nervous. Irma was lively and funny and some-times quite outrageous. Cornelia was the sensible one, skeptical of wild ideas. Hay Lin, so light and quick, was always in a good mood—or almost always. At the moment, she didn't look too happy.

When we were all together, there were jokes, mostly Irma's, and some teasing, and quite a lot of laughs. There was none of that now. My friends looked a little . . . I don't know, maybe a bit the way I felt: sort of hollow and sad. But not one of them said, *"I told you so."* Or: *"If only you hadn't been so stupid."* Or: *"This is all your fault."*

I joined them on the floor in a circle, locked hands with them, and closed my eyes. Please, I thought. Please hear us. I may have been hopelessly stupid and careless, but the other girls did not do anything to deserve this . . . this emptiness. Please.

There was a feeling of wind. A lightness. Something was definitely happening, but I didn't dare open my eyes.

Faintly, I heard a startled *Rrrrk!* from the dormouse and a faint "Good luck, Miss Will!" from James. Then, all the normal Heatherfield sounds—the distant rush and roar of traffic, the clicks and footsteps and TV noises from the other apartments—dropped away, and there was only silence.

"Welcome, Guardians."

I opened my eyes. Dimly, I was aware of the vast expanse of the Congregation Hall, of pillars almost infinitely high, and vaulted ceilings so far above us that they might as well have been sky. But the only thing I really saw was the Oracle's face.

There was no reproach in his eyes, only a

deep serenity and quiet expectation.

"I lost the Heart," I burst out, although I felt sure he already knew what I was going to say.

"Yes."

"I'll . . . I'll do anything to get it back!" I shouted.

"I hope not."

"What?" I asked in confusion. This was not what I had expected to hear.

"I hope you will do only what is needed and right."

I thought about that for a moment.

"I was . . . cheated," I said. And hurt. And humiliated. I didn't say the last two things out loud, but I was uncomfortably certain that he heard it all anyway.

"Yes."

"Danny *stole* the Heart," Irma said. "That's not right."

"It is unfortunate. And I regret your pain. But at this moment, the thief is in greater danger than you are."

"Danny? In danger?" Hay Lin asked.

"Yes."

I was the one who was hurting. Why would Danny be in danger?

"Do you think, Guardian, that someone can

hold the Heart of Candracar and not be changed by it?"

Thinking back to the moment when I had first held the Heart, I shook my head. No. It was true. Everything had changed—*everything*.

"And one who holds it unlawfully may be changed . . . dangerously. For that reason, too, you must win back the Heart."

"But . . . where is he? Who is he? " Cornelia asked. Hearing that Danny was in trouble now made the situation worse.

I looked around the circle at my friends. They were trying to piece together this mystery and bring our complete powers back.

"The answer to *what* is also the answer to *where*. He is on Nimbus, home of the Solar Salamanders."

"Danny is . . . a salamander?" Irma blurted out. "He seems more like a rat!"

"A Solar Salamander is a creature of energy. It can take almost any shape it pleases."

I suddenly remembered the very large cat with very blue eyes, watching us, spying on us . . . seeing me use the Heart. Had Danny been making plans all along to trick me? Pretending to like me, when all the time he . . . I felt hot tears on my face, and brushed them away angrily. How could I have fallen for that?

"Why did he steal it, if it's so dangerous?" Cornelia wondered aloud.

"How could he have come to Heatherfield, anyway? If he lives on this . . . this Nimbus world?" Hay Lin asked.

"As for how he came to your world . . . I have said that Salamanders can take almost any shape. A few—only a very talented few—may take no form at all, but travel as pure energy. And as light passes through glass, so they may pass from world to world."

I thought of what the blue radio had said: *He turned into a light.*

"How come we don't see more of them, then?" Taranee asked. She loved science, and I could tell that the factual inconsistency was bothering her. She needed more information.

"Because Salamanders are oath-bound. They are bound to serve and protect their region and their people. If Danny broke his oath to come to you, his peril is even greater than yours, and you must reach him quickly."

I thought the Oracle was displaying a lot of concern for a lying, cheating thief. After all, I was extremely angry. I wondered why the Oracle didn't seem mad. But, I thought, it didn't really matter. I was mad—and more than ready to fight.

"Can you send us there?" I asked, my attention returning to the Oracle.

"I will."

"How soon?" Irma inquired.

There was a smile on the Oracle's face. It was just like him to always seem one step ahead of us.

"Now, my impatient one. Now."

6

Zzziing. Karoooooom. Crash!

The weather in Nimbus was awful. Thunder crashed and boomed around us in the thick gloom and lightning split the charcoal sky.

Lightning . . . red lightning.

"So *that's* what he meant," I said, looking around.

"What?" muttered Cornelia.

"Er . . . nothing." I could feel my cheeks burning. "It's just . . . Danny told me that my hair was lightning-colored."

Taranee raised an eyebrow. "Well, at least we know we've come to the right place," she said, with a smile.

The lightning bolts that zapped incessantly across the sky were a pure, brilliant scarlet that turned to white only at the very core. They gave the place a festive air. It was if there were fire-works being set off. They were beautiful to watch—that is, until the first icy pieces of hail began to pelt us.

"Yikes!" The hail hit Taranee right on the top of the head.

"Ow!" yelled Irma, rubbing her forehead where she'd gotten hit. "Those things are *hard*!"

Not only were the hailstones hard; they were big. This wasn't just hail—it was like being shot with bullets of ice.

"We've got to find shelter," I yelled. "Look—there's some sort of light up ahead. Let's go there."

We stumbled on through the storm. Taranee and I linked arms to avoid being swept off our feet. The trail was slippery with sleet, and the low, mossy banks that rose on either side of it were studded with small, thorny bushes that did not like being touched. I know—I stumbled against one and got a stinging scratch on my arm.

When I looked up, I noticed a different glim-mer of light ahead of us. It did not look friendly.

Craaaaash. Zzzazzzzzinng!

Blinding light turned the air white for a moment, then scarlet, then black. I stumbled and fell to my hands and knees, on rock and rough gravel. I couldn't see at all!

Then, gradually, my vision began to come back. In front of us, no more than a few steps away, a stumpy-looking tree was burning. Lightning had split it right down the middle.

"That was close," muttered Irma in a shaky voice. "It isn't safe here."

I could feel the rumble of power overhead. I could feel the angry tension as another lightning bolt got ready to crackle. No place looked safe.

"You're right. It isn't safe," I said. "Not . . . not as we are now." Without the Heart, I meant, but I couldn't bear to say it out loud. "Unless Hay Lin can . . ." I wasn't quite sure what—blow away the storm? Ask the winds to take it elsewhere?

Hay Lin shook her head. "I already tried. But . . . I'm just not strong enough without . . ." she hesitated, but I guess she didn't want to talk about the Heart, either. "I'm just not strong enough," she repeated. She looked so small and cold and lost. Her straight black hair was absolutely plastered to her skull. All the same, she gave us a shaky smile. "I guess we just have to do what everyone else does—go indoors." She sneezed.

We kept on walking, all holding hands. We trudged through the storm, looking for the light that I had seen earlier, before the angry light had attacked. It felt like our only hope. Thunder continued to batter our eardrums, but at least the hail had stopped and had been replaced by icy rain—though I wasn't quite sure whether that was an improvement. The rain hurt less, but we sure got wetter.

Finally, we got close enough to see that the light we had followed came from the shuttered windows of a small—well, I suppose it was a farmhouse. It was partially dug into the hill behind it, and turf covered its roof so that it was hard to see where the hill left off and the house began. We let ourselves in through a white gate, crossed the wet, cobblestoned yard, and knocked on the door.

Almost at once, it was flung open.

"Come in, come in. . . ." roared a rumbly, bass voice. "Don't let all the heat out—" The speaker stopped abruptly. "Oh, my," he said. "What strange-looking company!"

Well, at least *we* didn't have horns, like the man who was facing us. It was on the tip of my tongue to say so, but I didn't. It wouldn't have been exactly polite. And really, they were quite handsome horns. Curled like a ram's and carefully polished and lacquered. Apart from that, and being rather woolly, this man looked almost human. Like a stocky, strong, short, middle-aged man.

"Excuse us," I said, "But we're strangers here, and we were hoping you would give us shelter from the storm—"

"Storm?" he looked startled. "Is there a storm coming on?" He all but pushed us out of the way to get a look at the sky. Then he sighed in relief. "Ah, no, that's nothing but a little squall. Be over in a few hours. Well, come on in, come on in, don't stand there getting wet."

A little squall? I was sure those hailstones had left bruises all over our bodies. But I wasn't about to argue with the man's welcoming invitation. We followed him through a tunnel-like hall into a big, cavernous kitchen.

"Mrs. Cuddlefleece," he called. "Mrs. Cuddlefleece, we've got company!"

A large creature—female, obviously, even if not human—turned from the cheerfully blazing hearth and the stewpan she had been stirring to take a startled look at the visitors her husband had brought into the house. At least, I assumed the horned beast was her husband.

"Oh, my," she said, just as he had. "And such wet company too! Mr. Cuddlefleece, don't just stand there. Get some robes and towels! Soap and hot water. The poor lambkins are positively drenched!"

"Um, we don't want to be any trouble—" I hesitantly began, but she brushed aside my objections.

"Nonsense. Now, get out of those wet things—what strange clothes to wear for out-doors! And get me that large tub from the scullery, there." She pointed with a dripping ladle.

Irma and Taranee went to obey her, looking as dazed as I felt. Trying not to stare too hard at our motherly hostess, I glanced around the room. From the dark rafters overhead hung nets full of roots and onions and dried fruits and berries. On shelves all around the walls sat cups, saucers, and handsomely painted platters, as well as enameled tins of varying sizes and shapes. We could almost have been in a very old-fashioned country kitchen back in Heatherfield. Except that the woman stirring the stew happened to have white, curly fleece over most of her body, or at least on the parts not covered by her blue dress and white apron. No horns, though. Maybe only the men of Nimbus had them.

Mr. Cuddlefleece came back bearing a large

pile of fluffy robes and towels. Hot water from a huge copper kettle was poured into the tub Taranee and Irma had fetched. It was large enough that two of us could fit in at once. Not too long after, we were all warm, clean, and wrapped in wonderfully soft, long, woolly robes.

"And now," said Mr. Cuddlefleece, "now, perhaps, you will tell us why you are here?"

"Over a hot meal," added Mrs. Cuddlefleece firmly, and ladled some creamy, white stew into seven earthenware bowls.

"Do you know a Salamander called Danny Nova?" I asked, hoping that Danny hadn't lied about his name, too.

"Nova?" repeated Mr. Cuddlefleece, and he rubbed his bearded, black chin. "There are a couple of Novas over Gloomsbury way, aren't there, Mrs. Cuddlefleece?"

"I believe there are," she said, filling his cup with cold cider. "But no Danny that I've heard of. That's not a Salamander name."

"Oh, and there was a Nova in Brambleton, once," added Mr. Cuddlefleece. He took a sip of his cider and looked as if he were trying to remember something else. "Don't know if he's still there, though. And yes, one Nova in Upper Smithwell."

My heart sank.

"The one we're looking for is about a little taller than me, has—" I stopped talking. I realized that giving a description of a shape-shifter was pointless. Salamanders could take almost any shape they wanted, the Oracle had said. Oh, no, I thought. We're never going to find him. What had I been thinking? I sniffed, trying to hold back a few hopeless tears.

I felt a soft, white-fleeced hand pat my arm.

"There, there, dear," said Mrs. Cuddlefleece gently. "It'll be all right. You'll see. What is it you want with this Nova of yours?"

The hand patting my arm had only four fingers. It made the whole experience a little unreal. But Mrs. Cuddlefleece's kindness was obviously genuine.

"He has . . . I lost . . . he stole . . ." I couldn't go on.

"Something of yours?" Her dark eyes were sympathetic. "Most Salamanders are good, you know. Even if a bit . . . sneaky. And we couldn't survive without them. Always remember that! But, when they see something they want . . . well, they're just not like us. I do hope you find what you're looking for, lambkin. In the meantime, you all need to eat!"

Mr. Cuddlefleece was right—the "squall" only lasted a few hours. Real storms, he said, could go on for days, and were much more ferocious. I hoped I wouldn't be on Nimbus long enough to witness one firsthand.

"Thanks for everything, Mrs. Cuddlefleece," said Irma as she gave our hostess a brief hug the next morning. "You're a lifesaver!"

"Well, yes, that may be," said Mrs. Cuddlefleece. "But you take care of yourselves, now. No gadding about in all weathers without a proper cloak!"

Proper cloaks were obviously high on her list of priorities, and, given the weather on Nimbus, one could see why. Due to her generosity, we were all warmly wrapped up now, in cloaks made from hastily altered blankets.

"Which way?" said Mr. Cuddlefleece, who had insisted on walking with us at least as far as the next town. "Toward Brambleton or toward Gloomsbury?"

"That way," I said instantly, pointing roughly east.

"Gloomsbury it is, then," he said, and turned right, out of the gate.

We walked a little while in silence.

"Why this way?" Taranee asked me.

"Don't know," I said. I looked at each of my friends. "It just . . . felt right."

"You sounded very certain," Hay Lin said.

"Did I?" I had been very certain, I realized. There'd been no hesitation at all.

"Oh," I said, stopping.

Cornelia nearly bumped into me. "What's the matter with you?" she asked, startled.

"I just . . ." I said. "I just realized. I *know*."

"What? You know what?" Irma asked, pulling at my arm.

I put a hand on my chest. "I can feel it. I can *feel* the Heart."

Just as a sunflower knows where the sun is, and a homing pigeon knows where to fly, I *knew*. I grinned crazily and felt like laughing for the first time since . . . well, since the Ghost Train. "He's not going to get away with this. I know where he is. He can run, but he can't hide. . . ." I said. I felt like doing a cartwheel, right there on the muddy track, I was so happy.

"Are you sure?" asked Cornelia.

I nodded.

"Well, great," Irma said, grinning. "Then, all we have to worry about is how to take the Heart away from him once we get to him."

There was a crack of thunder, and the sky suddenly grew darker.

"Girls," called Mr. Cuddlefleece. "You must hurry, now. There's another squall coming, and we need to reach the next shelter."

I looked at Irma. "And hope we don't get hit by lightning before we get there."

€ € ⚠ ◎ €

Rain was coming down so hard it seemed to form a solid sheet. The shelter that we were all huddled in was more a sort of hollow, dug into the hill. Mr. Cuddlefleece explained to us that there were such shelters along all reasonably traveled roads in Nimbus. It was helpful to have these safe places in which to rest and stay out of the wild storm.

As we waited for the latest storm to pass, I had to ask a question that had been bothering me since dinner the previous night. "What did Mrs. Cuddlefleece mean when she said that thing about . . . about not being able to survive without Salamanders?" I asked hesitantly.

Mr. Cuddlefleece brushed a bit of rainwater off his woolly head. His wet horns gleamed in the gloomy space.

"Where are you from?" he asked. His question was not unkind, but curious. "Aren't there

Salamanders where you live?"

I shook my head. "Danny was the first I've ever met."

"Who protects you from lightning, then?" Mr. Cuddlefleece asked.

"We have a . . ." I began, searching for the right words. "A sort of device that you put on houses. It's called a lightning rod."

"Ah," he said. "A protective charm. Well, those may work well enough for some, I suppose. But around here, we put our trust in a good Salamander."

Oh, I thought. Of course. Salamanders feed on electricity. They would be able to *eat* lightning. Consume it. And if the past twelve hours were anything to go by, lightning was certainly more than plentiful on Nimbus.

Mr. Cuddlefleece raised his head. "The squall's letting up," he said. "Better move on if we are to make a bit of headway before the next round."

Letting up? I looked at the still sheetlike rain, and then at my fellow Guardians. He called *this* letting up?

"Taranee . . ." I said in a small voice. "Could you do something about this? Like—keep us dry?"

"I'll try," she said gloomily. "But it's not easy. Nothing's easy now."

I knew she meant *now that we don't have the Heart,* and I felt guilty all over again.

"Maybe you'd better not, then," I said. "Maybe we had all better save our energy for . . . for when it's really needed."

And so we trudged into the rain with only Mrs. Cuddlefleece's blanket cloaks for protection. I was warmer than before, but I still had a chilled feeling.

How were we ever going to find Danny?

7

"Oh, no," I said wearily. "We need to go *that* way." I pointed to the northern fork in the road.

"Are you sure?" said Irma just as wearily. "I mean . . . we're nearly there."

We could actually see Gloomsbury in the distance, and it would have been so nice, so comfortably close, if that had been where Danny was. But, unfortunately, it wasn't.

"That way," I repeated.

"Well, if you're sure, lasses," said Mr. Cuddlefleece dubiously. "But that's the road to Lilypond, that is. I'm afraid you're on your own, then, or I won't be able to get back to Mrs. Cuddlefleece tonight."

"How far is it to Lilypond?" asked Cornelia skeptically.

"Oh, at least another half day's journey, given

that the weather stays as good as we've had. Why don't you go see the Gloomsbury Salamander, now that you're here? She might know more about your Danny Nova than I do. I believe she is a Nova, herself. Solana, her name is."

It sounded a lot more attractive than slogging another umpteen miles in the mud—especially if my instinct proved to be wrong. But it wasn't. I knew without a doubt it wasn't.

"Can't hurt to ask," said Hay Lin matter-of-factly. "Now that we're here."

Mr. Cuddlefleece took us past the town— almost all made up of low, turf-covered houses like his own, I noticed—to what he referred to as the Salamander Tower, just north of the town. Well, at least it was in the right general direction, I thought, impatiently. As we began to trudge up the hill to the Gloomsbury Salamander's lofty doorstep, there was yet another massive boom, and a crackle of electricity overhead.

Mr. Cuddlefleece stopped in his tracks. "Oops," he said. "Up or down, lasses? Decide quickly, please; to be caught halfway is not a good idea."

"Up," I answered immediately. "If we go down we'll only have to climb it again later."

"Well, then, let's hope our Salamander is

doing her job," he said, casting a wary eye skyward.

Scarlet lightning blazed across the sky. The air was so heavy with static that Mr. Cuddlefleece's woolly coat frizzed. At least it wasn't raining at the moment, I thought. And then I caught sight of something that nearly took my breath away.

It was huge, white, and absolutely breathtaking. The creature looked like a dragon, with a long neck and enormous, billowing wings. And it had a glow like that of a bright star against a midnight sky. The creature was soaring, swooping, and spinning playfully on currents of air.

More lightning crackled across the sky. I had a vague memory of science class and Benjamin Franklin's kite. The creature was so high, so huge, that I wondered how it could *not* be struck?

Bright crimson lines of light zigzagged around the creature. The white wings seemed to spread further and further. The lightning struck, once, twice, and the creature was drawn to it, beating those wings against the ruby-colored streaks.

I think I cried out.

Mr. Cuddlefleece laughed, a booming sound of pure relief. "Ah, there she is," he said. "Well, we should be safe enough now." And he merely continued up the hill.

I was still waiting fearfully to see the magnificent creature up there char and burn and fall to earth. It didn't. It soared still higher. And then I realized what Mr. Cuddlefleece had been talking about. The creature was the Gloomsbury Salamander, of course. She was doing her job. She was ingesting the lightning.

We reached the tower at the top of the hill. It was by far the tallest building around—the only tall building, in fact. That made sense, I supposed. To build something tall in that place would have been to invite lightning to strike, and no one but a Salamander would have wanted to do that.

Mr. Cuddlefleece knocked on the tower gate and then went in. The Salamander was still up there soaring, though apparently no one else was around. We climbed a spiral staircase to a large, bare room at the top. In the middle of it roared a fire, in a wide, round, stone hearth. On a shelf running around half the room was an odd collection of objects—some glass lenses of varying sizes; a small, toy windmill; an amulet of some kind; and what looked like some lumps of coal. Despite the fire, it was cold up there, from the breeze coming through a large, arched doorway that led out onto a balcony.

"It's freezing in here," said Hay Lin, teeth chattering. "When will she return?"

"When she's dealt with the squall," said Mr. Cuddlefleece. "Might not be too long. It's just a little one."

I had started to realize that what we considered "little," with respect to storms, was not the same as Mr. Cuddlefleece's conception of littleness.

It was not much longer before the glowing white creature alighted on the balcony, shrunk a bit, solidified, and disappeared behind the wall. A moment later, a very large, white wolf padded into the room.

"Oh," said the wolf, catching sight of us. "Sorry. One moment."

There was a blur of light, so blinding I had to close my eyes, and then a feeling of intense heat. When I opened my eyes again, a stately Nimbus woman, about the size of Mrs. Cuddlefleece but much more elegant, stood where the wolf had crouched a moment before.

"I didn't realize I had visitors," said the Salamander. "I don't get many."

Was there just a tinge of loneliness in that voice? There was something strange about a creature that *fed* on lightning. Three transformations in as many minutes left all of us uncertain as to whom or what we were actually talking to in the tower. But I thought the Gloomsbury Salamander had been beautiful out there, against the slate-dark sky, and there was a feeling of *life* about her that reminded me of—Danny.

"Good Nooning, Madam Solana," said Mr. Cuddlefleece. "These lasses have traveled far to come here, to make inquiries about someone who might be a relative of yours."

"Oh?" she said, watching us in turn. She had not changed her eyes, I noticed—they were still the predatory yellow of the wolf, all iris and no whites. "And who might that be?"

"He called himself Danny," I said hesitantly. "But I don't know whether that was his real name."

She knew him. I could tell right away. But she didn't let on at first.

"That is not a Salamander name," she said, just as Mrs. Cuddlefleece had said.

"Please, Madam Solana. He has taken something that belongs to me, something that is dangerous to him. We must get it back. For his sake as much as for ours."

"So. What is this dangerous thing?" she asked, her wolf's eyes steady on my face.

I couldn't tell her. *A Salamander who sensed*

the Heart would long to hold it. The Oracle's voice was in my head. I suddenly understood. I didn't want to exchange one Salamander thief for another.

"It's just . . . a keepsake," I mumbled, ill at ease. "But it was given to me by someone important, and it is rightfully mine."

"And now you want it back," she said.

"Yes," I whispered.

She looked at me for what felt like a very long time, her yellow eyes unreadable. Then she bowed her head. "I cannot help you," she said.

Mr. Cuddlefleece's hand had closed around my elbow in a very strong grip. "Madam Solana is tired from her flight," he said urgently. "We must not intrude any longer."

The Salamander's woman-shape had begun to flicker. Little strands of light were unraveling from the curly white fleece that looked so like Mrs. Cuddlefleece's. And the yellow eyes glowed even more golden than before.

"I cannot help you," she repeated, and her voice sounded strained. "Please leave."

"At once, Madam." Mr. Cuddlefleece all but hustled us out the door and down the steps. "Run," he said in a constrained voice. "Get off the hill. Now!"

There was such urgency in his voice that we didn't stop to question him. We just ran. Halfway down the hill, there was an explosion of light behind us, and the ground shook. An angry keening seemed to make every bone in my skull vibrate—like a dentist's drill, only worse. And there was a word in that keening. A name.

Halidan!

Was that Danny's real name? I thought it must be.

There was a dry rush of huge, white wings above us. I ducked my head, but we weren't the Salamander's intended target. Riding the wind, she spiraled, higher and higher. And then she took off, in the direction of Lilypond.

"Ah," said Mr. Cuddlefleece, slowly getting up. "I am very sorry, lasses. I'm afraid I gave you bad advice."

I thought so, too. It didn't take much in the way of brains to figure out that Madam Solana was chasing after Danny. And from the sound of that screech, her intentions were far from friendly.

"I created this trouble for you," said Mr. Cuddlefleece. "The least I can do is help you get out of it."

"But what about Mrs. Cuddlefleece? You

won't be home by nightfall like you promised."

He sighed. "Mrs. Cuddlefleece will understand. Now, do you want to go to Lilypond, or don't you?"

"We do," said Cornelia. "And quickly, too. I'm freezing."

We were, Mr. Cuddlefleece told us later, exceedingly lucky with the weather. What this meant was that we only had to take cover twice on the half-day trudge to Lilypond. All the same, the cold mud squelching around our ankles got colder, and our tired legs got tireder. I envied Madam Solana her wings. She would get there long before we did, and that thought made me very uneasy.

As we neared Lilypond, we began to meet quite a few people leaving it. Mr. Cuddlefleece spoke quietly with one family all of whose belongings appeared to be loaded onto a low wagon drawn by two disgruntled-looking steers.

"House burned down," said the man, rubbing his horns in frustration. "What could we do? Didn't want to build a new one in a place where the Salamander's not fit to do his job. Waste of time, and dangerous, too. We've got kin over Upper Smithwell way. Thought we'd go there."

His wife was trying to comfort one of their

children, a small, woolly boy who was mewling in fatigue.

"There, there, lambkin," she hummed. "There, there." She sounded so exactly like Mrs. Cuddlefleece that I got an odd pang of homesickness for the small, turf-covered farmhouse where I had spent only one night.

Lilypond was a sorry sight. Hardly a tree was standing, and many houses had been burned completely to the ground, while others had large, charred patches in the roof. Mr. Cuddlefleece clicked his tongue in disapproval.

"Well, here we are," he said. "Such as it is. The Salamander Tower should be up that-there way." He pointed north. "Do you want to get a meal first? Not good, facing whatever you'll be facing on an empty stomach."

I shook my head. I could feel the Heart now, so strongly it hurt, like an ache inside, somewhere close to my own beating heart. I couldn't bear to wait any longer.

"Well, what do we do?" said Irma. "We can't just go up there, bang on his door, and demand that he give us the Heart back. Or can we?"

One part of me wanted to rush up and do just that. Anything, anything, just so that I could be whole again. But I thought of the Oracle's words:

I hope you will do only what is needed and right. And then I thought of the way Madam Solana had looked just before we ran from her tower. Without the Heart, I felt hopelessly weak. I wasn't sure I wanted to stand between her and anything she wanted without the power of the Heart. I rubbed my aching chest with a cold hand.

"Maybe we need to take a good look at what we're getting into, first," I said. "We're not going to be able just to flatten any resistance with magic, after all."

"We can't even transform ourselves," said Cornelia gloomily. "Much as I'd love to get out of these wet rags. We're pretty much stuck being our normal selves."

"Well," said Irma determinedly. "It's a good thing we're not just magic and good looks— remember, we're pretty clever, too!"

I couldn't help smiling at Irma's remark. With the exception of Cornelia, who managed to make the homemade blanket-cloak look like a cutting-edge fashion accessory, we were a ragged-looking lot: chilled, wet, dirty, and, if I was anything to go by, thoroughly scared.

"Great," I said. "All this and brains, too. How can we lose?"

Taranee smiled grimly. Hay Lin, surely feeling colder than any of us, being by far the lightest, produced a cheerful grin, though her teeth were chattering wildly.

"This will make a great story when we get back home," she said.

"Yeah," said Cornelia. "Too bad we can't actually tell anyone."

The Salamander Tower was very high above the town of Lilypond, on what was almost a mountain ridge. There was a road leading to it, or rather, a cart track—two muddy ruts that seemed more to be a way for water to go downhill than a way for people to go uphill. Someone had apparently given up on the project already: an abandoned cart, with one wheel broken, sat beside the track, like a patient dog waiting for its owner to come back.

We began to climb, slipping and sliding in the mud on the steepest parts. Mr. Cuddlefleece kept looking up at the sky anxiously, but for once it seemed clear and almost springlike.

"Nearly there," he said. "Do you want to—"

He never finished his question.

There was a wave of blinding light, and a huge, echoing boom. All of us were flung flat on our backs, and for a moment I could do nothing except lie there, flat in the mud, ears ringing and the breath knocked out of me.

Boom! Boom! Boom!

A series of sharp cracks, almost like gunshots, followed. For just an instant I saw the stark, square tower, black against a sky completely scarlet with sheets of lightning. Then I felt Mr. Cuddlefleece's strong hand jerking me to my feet.

"Run, girl," he said. "Run for your life. That's a Salamander storm." His wide nostrils flared red, and a ring of panicked white circled his normally placid dark eyes. I had absolutely no doubt that he thought it was run or die.

I didn't want to. I stood rooted to the spot, chest aching, wanting only one thing: to go up, grasp the Heart, and wrest it from the one who had taken it.

Mr. Cuddlefleece was not having any of that. His head came down so quickly that for a moment I thought he would actually butt me with his horns, but instead he rammed his shoulder against my middle, wrapped an arm around my legs, and swung me up so that I hung head down across his wide, strong back.

"There's a shelter at the foot of the trail," he shouted. "Run, lasses. Get there!"

Next to the path, a small spruce tree suddenly caught fire in a rush of flames. The air was filled with sparks and burning needles. A roar of wind came down the hill, causing Mr. Cuddlefleece to stumble on to his knees, but he still managed to keep hold of me.

"Let me go," I cried. "I'll run. I promise I'll run."

I was slowing him down. He wouldn't make it, I wouldn't make it, unless we both used every ounce of speed we had. He hardly seemed to hear me. I beat frantically at his back with my fists, and then there was another blast of wind, even fiercer than the first.

He stumbled again, cried out in pain, and this time had to let me go. I fell forward, facedown in mud that was no longer cold, but steaming. There was no time to count the bruises and tender spots. I rolled, got to my feet, and frantically looked around for Mr. Cuddlefleece.

He lay on his hands and feet in the mud, gasping for air.

"Run," he rasped. "Girl, will you run?"

"Not without you," I told him. Irma was at my side now, trying to get his other arm around her shoulders.

"Please, get up, Mr. Cuddlefleece," she cried.

Fire was coming down the hill in little rivers, leaping from tuft to tuft of grass, and from bush to bush. Thunder split the air.

"Can't, lass," said Mr. Cuddlefleece. "Ankle's gone. You're going to have to leave me here."

"No," I said. "No way! Taranee, you have to hold back the fire!"

Taranee looked grim. She knew there was not much she could do without the full power of the Heart.

"Cornelia, you're supposed to be able to move solid objects," Irma said. "Mr. Cuddlefleece is as solid as they get!"

Cornelia blanched. "But he's alive," she said. "I don't know that I can move something that's living. Plus, we haven't got the Heart!"

"Move something else, instead, then," said Hay Lin. "Move that abandoned cart we saw. I'll help and try to make it lighter."

"But quickly, please," I said.

"Girls," said Mr. Cuddlefleece, in a voice oddly frantic and weary at the same time, "Don't. Leave me. Save yourselves."

"And you!" I said, turning back to him. "If you think I have any intention of telling Mrs. Cuddlefleece that we left you on a burning hill-side in the middle of a . . . of a Salamander storm, you have another think coming."

He looked at me with a startled expression, as if he had never expected a "lambkin" to talk to him like that. He opened his mouth, then closed it again.

With a thump and a rattle, the broken cart arrived beside us.

"We did it!" said Cornelia. And then she stumbled and sat down suddenly, clutching her temples. "Ouch! My head!"

Hay Lin looked only a little better, pale and panting. But I had no time for that.

"Taranee! How are you doing?"

"Just hurry!" she said through clenched teeth, heading off another gust of flame and sending it off to one side of the track. Sweat was trickling down her face and dripping from the ends of her braids, and her glasses were crooked.

"Irma," I said. "Help me get Mr. Cuddlefleece onto the cart."

"What about the broken wheel?" Taranee asked, pointing to the cart.

I tried to jam it on more firmly. I wasn't sure it did much good. "We'll just have to hold the cart steady between us," I said out loud. "Anyway, it's downhill."

We got Mr. Cuddlefleece onto—well, not onto

his feet, because one dangled uselessly and looked badly broken—but onto his one good foot. Supported by Irma and me, he hopped to the cart and slid onto it with a heavy sigh.

"Irma, can you help Taranee?" I asked. "She can't watch the fire *and* see where she's going."

"Sure," said Irma. "I might be able to put out a few fires, too."

Thunder boomed again. The hill shook beneath our feet.

"Hay Lin, Cornelia, I know you're tired, but you really have to help with the cart." I called over my shoulder.

Hay Lin nodded wearily and went to one side of the cart. Cornelia was still sitting on the track, clutching her head.

"Cornelia?" I said.

"Go away," she muttered. "My head really *hurts*."

She had pushed herself, getting that cart to us. There was nothing left, no strength, no energy. . . .

Energy. Well, that was supposed to be my field, wasn't it?

"Cornelia," I said, walking over to her. "I have a gift for you."

Surprised, she looked up. I put a hand on

either side of her face. And I gave her strength.

Then I touched Hay Lin's tired face. Then Irma's. Then Taranee's. My own shoulders sagged. A small, pounding pain was starting up behind my temples. Meanwhile, Cornelia had gotten slowly to her feet and looked a little less pained.

"What did you do that for?" she said. "Now we're *both* tired."

"Yeah," I said. "But only half as much."

♦ ♦ ♦ ♦ ♦

The winds roared, and the thunder hammered at us. Fire swept the hill. But we managed to get down—all of us together.

This shelter, too, was little more than a hole in the hillside. But it was cover from the hailstorms and the scarlet lightning. It was even, almost, dry.

We had no food and only one bottle of luke-warm water among us. We shared it. Then all we could do was wait.

"How is your ankle?" I asked Mr. Cuddle-fleece.

"Still broken," he grunted. "But it will heal. Now that you've given it the chance. Thank you, lasses."

I smiled. "Any time." Then a yawn caught me. "As long as it's not any time soon."

I couldn't remember when I had last felt so tired. My chest hurt. More than an ache now, it was a deep, desperate pain. If that storm didn't stop soon, I'd either have to walk right into it or tell the others to hold me down so that I didn't. I wanted my Heart back. It was very nearly all I could think of.

"What's a Salamander storm?" asked Irma, curiosity surfacing even through her exhaustion.

"A storm made by a Salamander," said Mr. Cuddlefleece simply. "It usually only happens when they fight each other."

I listened to the roar of fire and the tremors of the hill. "Do they do that often?"

He smiled tiredly. "No. Almost never. If they did it more often, Nimbus would be a wasteland."

Danny must have been fighting Solana, and I desperately wanted to know who was winning.

8

It was nearly dawn before the vicious winds eased and the shattering cracks of thunder stopped. Some of the others had slept a little. I had not. The pain in my chest had kept me wide awake.

"I'm going up," I said to Taranee, quietly, so I wouldn't wake the slumbering Mr. Cuddlefleece.

"I'll come with you," she said quickly.

"We're all coming with you," Irma said.

"You don't have to," I told my friends. "You've done enough." Without Taranee and Irma, we definitely wouldn't have gotten off the hill unburned. Without Cornelia and Hay Lin, we couldn't have saved Mr. Cuddlefleece. We'd already fought one battle. How could I drag them into another so soon?

"Aren't you the one who's always telling us

that we're stronger and more powerful together?" Hay Lin asked, with a tired smile.

"Yes," I said. "I guess I am."

"Well, then?" Cornelia sighed.

"Yes. All right," I said. "Let's go."

We ducked out of the shelter, leaving Mr. Cuddlefleece still sleeping, unaware of what we were about to do. The countryside was almost unrecognizable. On the once-green hillside, nothing lived. All was blackened, charred, pitted with lightning scars. . . .

"What a depressing sight," said Irma.

"Mmm . . ." I sighed in acknowledgment. "Let's get going."

Whichever Salamander had won would be tired after that battle, I thought. But more tired than we were? We could barely walk; how were we going to fight, let alone fight a Salamander? Yet, putting one foot in front of another, we did walk. Maybe the strength to fight would come also, when we really needed it.

We climbed the last incline. Above us rose the Salamander Tower, square, dark, and forbidding. And then I came to an abrupt stop.

On the steps leading up to the tower crouched a huge, white wolf, watching us steadily, with a grim, unblinking, yellow gaze.

"It's her," I hissed. "It's Madam Solana. I guess . . . I guess that means she won."

What had become of Danny? What had become of the Heart?

It was there. In the tower. I could feel it.

I took another step forward and stood as tall as I could.

"Let us pass," I told Solana. "We won't hurt you if you'll just let us pass."

My arms felt as if they were about to fall off. My chest felt on fire. I had half a dozen scratches, bruises, and small burns, and no energy left at all. I couldn't have hurt her even if I had wanted to, but I was hoping she wouldn't know that. Slowly, I raised my hands. I knew the others, spread out in a semicircle behind me, had done the same.

The wolf rose. She growled. Her white fur looked less than pristine, almost ashen. She yawned, staring me right in the face. And then she slunk away, leaving the steps to the tower open and free.

I couldn't believe it.

"It . . . it worked!" I exclaimed.

"Apparently," said Cornelia. "Unless it's a trap?"

"There's only one way to find out," I said, not

willing to wait even a minute longer. If I had had the energy, I would have rushed up those steps. The Heart was so near now I felt I could just reach out and take it.

At the top of the steps was a room much like Solana's—circular fireplace, trophy shelf, door, and balcony. But where was the Heart? I looked around wildly.

Danny came through the balcony doorway.

I froze. Danny? But I thought Solana had . . .

"I thought you'd lost," I burst out.

"No," he said, not smiling. "I won." He grimaced with what seemed like sour satisfaction. "She won't be able to shape-shift for a while. She'll have to limp on home wearing that old wolf guise all the way."

There was something different about him. Not physically, perhaps—he wore the form I knew, the strong, square shoulders, the auburn hair, the eyes. But something else was changed.

And then I realized what it was. The joy had gone out of him.

"I am very strong now," he told me. "Stronger than before. I don't think you could fight me and win."

"Try me," I said, angrily, even though I knew that he was probably right. He had the Heart. I didn't. He had defeated Solana, who had sent us all running back at the Salamander Tower in Gloomsbury.

"Only if you make me," he said. "I've grown rather—tired of fighting." He rubbed his forehead. "Solana was the third in two days. She was by far the strongest of the three, of course, but I am stronger than anyone, now."

I took a step forward. He eyed me warily.

"Give me back the Heart," I said.

"Why?" he asked. He stood very tall and strong.

Why? I couldn't believe that he could ask me that. "Because it isn't yours," I finally said.

"It is now," he replied.

"No," I said. I felt the power of my friends beside me. "You may hold it, but I am its Keeper."

"You didn't keep it too well, did you?" Danny chuckled.

That stung. "You cheated me. You lied to me," I said to him. "You said you *liked* me." I was very tired, and everything hurt, my chest worst of all. Otherwise I might not have said the last few words.

He actually looked away for a moment. Could there be a conscience in a Salamander?

"For what it's worth," Danny said very softly,

"I didn't lie about liking you."

"Well, isn't that sweet?" muttered Cornelia sarcastically.

"That didn't stop you from robbing me!" I cried. Angrily, I took another step forward.

"Hold it," he said. "Don't come any closer. I don't want to fight you, Will, but if I must. . . ."

Pain like a knife blade tore through me. I went down on one knee, then fell forward on the cold stone floor.

"Will!" Taranee cried, and ran to me, trying to lift me up. Irma was on the other side of me in a flash.

"Will," Irma hissed fiercely, "What's wrong? Did he hurt you?"

My eyes stung, but there was no way I was going to cry in front of that creep. I fought my way onto my knees and blinked angrily, fighting back my tears.

Danny was on his knees, too. He was wearing the same expression of pain that was no doubt on my face.

"It hurts," he said, softly.

And for a moment I saw a hint of the old Danny. The sweet boy with the beautiful eyes.

"Will, why does it hurt?" he pleaded.

"It isn't yours," I managed to say, through

clenched teeth. "You have to give it up. It will destroy you if you don't."

"But it's so powerful," he said, in a strangely childish voice. "They all want it. Solana said she saw it first; she was the one who told me it existed. But she couldn't go get it, could she? I did that. I was the one who found out how. And now they all keep coming to try and take it from me." For a moment his face twisted, ugly with fury. "You, too! You want to take it, too."

And suddenly I knew that that wasn't what I wanted at all.

"No," I whispered. "I won't take it from you. But if you give it to me, I will accept it."

That seemed to take him aback—and the others, too, for that matter.

"Will! You can't let him have it!" said Irma, aghast.

I steeled myself against the pain, and nodded.

"Yes. I can. It has to be that way. Don't you see? *It can't be taken.* The Heart can be given and accepted, but if you take it by force, both the taker and the one it is taken from may be destroyed."

There was a deadly silence in the chill, bare room.

"Destroyed?" said Danny, hesitantly.

"Yes. Isn't it destroying you?" I asked. "Isn't it destroying the Salamanders, and the world they are meant to protect?"

"The Heart wouldn't do that," said Taranee. "Not to us!"

"It's not the Heart that's doing it. It's us. Because our actions change us. As Danny's actions are changing him. You used to smile all the time, Danny. You used to be the happiest person I'd ever met. Are you happy now?"

"No," he said, very quietly. He sat back on his heels, hugging himself as if something inside him hurt. "Is it . . . destroying you?" he asked softly. "I never meant to do that, Will. I swear."

I wanted to believe him. I think, deep down, I did. There was no evil in Danny. Only mischief and too much curiosity.

"Can you give me back the Heart?" I asked him.

For a moment, his face shimmered, as if he meant to shape-shift. Then it became firm.

"I . . . no. I can't, Will." He hugged himself even harder. "It's too powerful," he whispered, with such longing in his voice he nearly made me cry in spite of myself.

I got to my feet, wondering how long a person could go on hurting as much as I did right then.

"Come on," I said to the others. "There's nothing more we can do."

"But you're not just . . . you're not just going to walk away from him," said Hay Lin. "You're not just going to leave it with him!"

"Yes, I am," I said.

And I started down the stairs. I had done what was right. And it hadn't been enough.

I was halfway down the stairs before he stopped me.

"Will!" Danny called.

I paused, but I didn't turn around. "Yes?"

"Please, may I," his voice was weak and tentative. ". . . May I give you something?"

Almost at once there was an easing of the pain in my chest, as if the Heart were already home again.

"Yes," I said. "You certainly may."

Given. Accepted. Never taken.

"Only . . ." he went on, coyly. "If I do . . . will you repair my CD player for me?"

Tired as I was, that made me laugh.

"I'll see what I can do," I said.

ⓔ ⓔ ⓐ ⓞ ⓒ

That wasn't quite the end of it, of course. We still had to repair the cart and take poor Mr. Cuddlefleece back to Mrs. Cuddlefleece. The weather was still lousy. We all caught colds. But as we prepared to leave Lilypond, we suddenly heard an energetic bass boom that wasn't thunder.

"I got the power, I got the moves," sang the voice of JoeJoe, a million miles from home. *"I got the music, I got the grooves. . . ."*

I laughed. Up there, in his tower room, I bet Danny was dancing. I hoped he was smiling, too.

"Well, I'm glad somebody's happy," said Cornelia grouchily.

"Aren't you?" I asked.

Her frown slipped. A smile poked through.

"Yeah," she said. "Things are *much* better now." She raised a casual hand, and on the burnt hillside, the trees were suddenly green again. Her smile grew wider. "Now, *that's* more like it!"

"Are you feeling all right now, Will?" asked Taranee, still looking a little worried. "For a moment up there, when you . . . when you just fell down like that . . ."

"I feel fine," I said. Well, more than fine, actually. I thought for a moment, and then I figured out the reason. It might not have been the kind of expression one usually used around school, but it fit my mood exactly. "You know how I feel?" I asked my friends. "I feel free at heart."

€ € ◭ ◉ €